We're Going on a
Ghost Hunt

Thanks to Nikki for joining me
on this ghost hunt.
—K.H.

For Oliver and Harper
—B.L.

ISBN 978-0-545-34173-8

12 11 10 9 8 7 6 5 4 3 2   11 12 13 14 15 16/0
Printed in the U.S.A.   40
First printing, October 2011

Book design by Kevin Callahan

We're Going on a Ghost Hunt

We're go-ing on a ghost hunt. We're gon-na see some spoo-ky o

We're not scared. It's Hal-lo-ween night!

Uh-oh! A for-est! An old, cold for-est

Can't go ov-er it. Can't go un-der it. W

have to go through it. Crunch! Crunch! Crunch!

We went on a ghost hunt.
We saw some spooky ones.
I wasn't scared. . . .

Were you?

Up the front path!
Into the house!
Slam the door!
WE MADE IT!

Through the forest!
Crunch! Crunch! Crunch!

Through the swamp!
Squish! Squish! Squish!

Across the bridge!
Creak! Creak! Creak!

Out of the haunted house!
Stomp! Stomp! Stomp!

Tiptoe,
tiptoe . . .
Uh-oh!
What's that??

We'll have to go into it.

Uh-oh! A haunted house!
An eerie, dreary haunted house!
Can't go over it.
Can't go under it.

Creak! Creak! Creak!
We made it!

Uh-oh! A bridge!
A freaky, squeaky bridge!
Can't go over it.
Can't go under it.
We'll have to go across it.

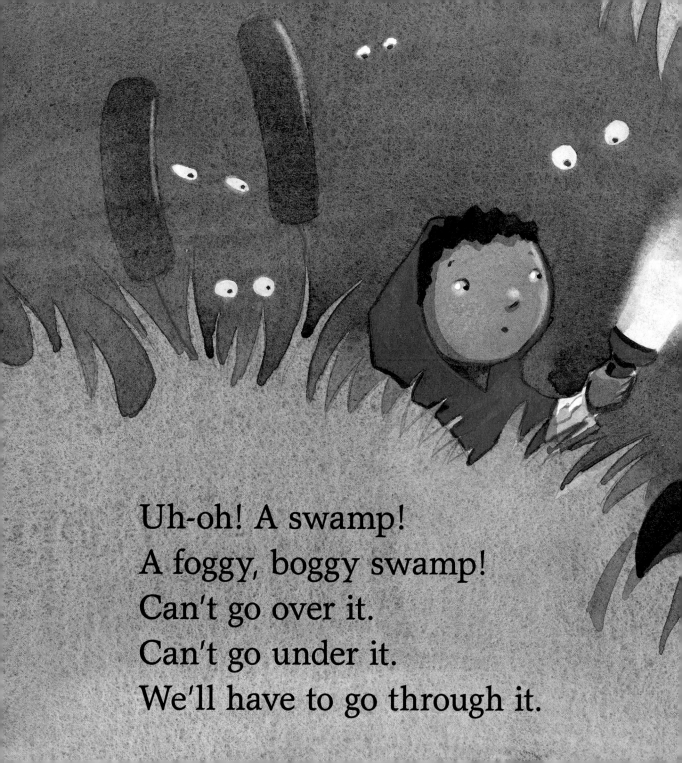

Uh-oh! A swamp!
A foggy, boggy swamp!
Can't go over it.
Can't go under it.
We'll have to go through it.

Crunch! Crunch! Crunch!
We made it!

Uh-oh! A forest!
An old, cold forest!
Can't go over it.
Can't go under it.
We'll have to go through it.

We're going on a ghost hunt.
We're gonna see some spooky ones.
We're not scared.
It's Halloween night!

SING AND READ STORYBOOK™

We're Going on a
Ghost Hunt

Adapted by Kris Hirschmann
Illustrated by Bryan Langdo

Scholastic Inc.
New York Toronto London Auckland
Sydney Mexico City New Delhi Hong Kong